Zain Bhikha

Cotton Candy Sky

The Song Book

Illustrated by Amir Al-Zubi

THE ISLAMIC FOUNDATION

Cotton Candy Sky: The Song Book

First Published in 2019 by
The Islamic Foundation

Distributed by
Kube Publishing Ltd
MCC, Ratby Lane, Markfield
Leicestershire, LE67 9SY
United Kingdom
Tel: +44 (0)1530 249230, Fax +44 (0)1530 249656
E-Mail: info@kubepublishing.com
Website: **www.kubepublishing.com**

Text and Lyrics © Zain Bikha
Illustrations © Amir Al-Zubi
Edited by Azra Momin and Johara Mansura
Story concept by Amir Al-Zubi and Meliha Cicak
Illustrator and Book Design by Amir Al- Zubi

In partnership with zeebee KIDS

www.zeebeekids.com & ™ Zain Bikha Studios

Zeebee Kids, A division of Zain Bikha Studios

A Catalogue-in-Publication Data record is available from the British Library

ISBN 978-0-86037-772-6

Printed in Istanbul by IMAK

For Zaydaan Bhikha...
my Cotton Candy Sky!

Allah has given me a Cotton Candy Sky
A little bit of blue, pink, purple and white

I sometimes see the grey and I sometimes feel the rain

But I'll see the colours of the Cotton Candy Sky again

I see the **red** of my **mother's** love

The true **blue** of my **father's** hugs

I see the **orange** of my **sibling's** smile
I see the **pink** and the **white** of the **love** of my life

And the deep, deep **green** that all **children** bring

Are the coolness of my **eyes**

For Allah has given me a Cotton Candy Sky
A little bit of blue, pink, purple and white

I sometimes see the grey and I sometimes feel the rain

But I'll see the colours of the Cotton Candy Sky again

الله تَوَكَّلْتُ عَلَيْكَ نُورٌ

Whenever I am down, I **look up** to the sky

And I see the signs from **Allah**, Most **High**

Most of all I see **Light**, endless Light upon Light

Mercy from **Allah** who is yours and mine

بسم الله الرحمن الرحيم رب العالمين

Al Rahman Al Raheem Rabb Al Aalameen

Bismillah and again I begin

Allah has given me a Cotton Candy Sky

A little bit of blue, pink, purple and white

I sometimes see the grey and I sometimes feel the rain

ut I'll see the colours of the Cotton Candy Sky again

I see the yellow like a sunflower smile

Of an orphan girl who says Alhamdulillah

Or a **mother** who lost her child

Sees them waiting on a throne of **gold**, so high

Or a **father** who holds his stride

Working hard everyday and is firm in his **faith**

Burning bright like a beautiful crimson flame

Says, Allah keep my family safe

الْحَمْدُ لِلَّه

For Allah has given me a Cotton Candy Sky
A little bit of blue, pink, purple and white

I sometimes see the grey and I sometimes feel the rain
But I'll see the colours of the Cotton Candy Sky again

Whenever I am down, I look up to the sky
And I see the signs from **Allah**, Most **High**

Most of all I see Light, endless Light upon Light

Mercy from Allah who is yours and mine

Al Rahman Al Raheem Rabb Al Aalameen

Bismillah and again I begin

Of course there are **times**

Both yours and mine

When the **tears** in our **eyes**

Sting and blur out the **light**

But these **lows** bring the **highs**
of the **strength** I have inside
to always see my
Cotton Candy Sky

For Allah has given me a Cotton Candy Sky
A little bit of blue, pink, purple and white

I sometimes see the grey and I sometimes feel the rain
But I'll see the colours of the Cotton Candy Sky again

About Zain Bhikha

Zain Bhikha has served as an inspiration to people the world over since he first began his career as an islamic artist in 1994. He is well-loved by fans young and old and remains amongst the most popular Islamic artists.

With more than a dozen albums to his name, Zain's songs have graced homes throughout the world and touched people's lives in uplifting and often profound ways. He has been described as an influential global peace and unity ambassador.

Zain's loyal fans have followed his career over more than 25 years and his audience continues to grow in his country of birth, South Africa as well as globally. His albums have been launched in all major cities and he has performed across most continents.

The song-book, "Cotton Candy Sky" is the second in a series of printed and illustrated books under Zain Bhikha's "ZeeBee Kids" label. Zain's passion for teaching and uplifting the lives of young children towards God-consciousness has been at the centre of many of his albums, plays and youth workshops. The natural evolution to print, live shows, Apps and other media forums under the exciting ZeeBee kids umbrella is yet another way that Zain remains a pioneer in his field.

Zain Bhikha resides in Johannesburg, South Africa where he enjoys spending quality time with his wife and four sons

About Amir and Meliha Al-Zubi

Al-Zubis, Amir and Meliha are a married couple and parents of five. They enjoy being storytellers through children's books and animation, promoting freedom and entrepreneurship. You can find some of their recent work on Instagram @simplegears.